**This Topsy and Tim
book belongs to**

_____

Topsy and Tim
Go to the Zoo

By Jean and Gareth Adamson

Illustrations by Belinda Worsley

A catalogue record for this book is available from the British Library

Published by Ladybird Books Ltd
A Penguin Company
Penguin Books Ltd., 80 Strand, London WC2R 0RL, UK
Penguin Books Australia Ltd., 707 Collins Street, Melbourne, Victoria 3008, Australia
Penguin Group (NZ) 67 Apollo Drive, Rosedale, North Shore 0632, New Zealand

010

ISBN: 978-1-40930-084-7
Printed in China

www.topsyandtim.com

Topsy and Tim were going to the zoo. First they
made sure their pets had all they needed for their day at home.
"Let's ask the zoo animals if they would like to come home
with us," said Topsy.
"Animals can't answer questions!" said Tim.

Topsy and Tim met
the penguins first.
They walked like funny
old men but they dived
and swam beautifully.

Topsy and Tim would have liked the penguins to come home with them but they looked so happy in the zoo.

The parrots in the aviary were making a dreadful noise.
Topsy had heard that parrots could answer questions,
so she asked one, "Would you like to come home with us?"
"Ripe bananas, brown bread," squawked the parrot.
"I'm afraid parrots don't give sensible answers," said Dad.

They went to see the friendly elephant.
"He's the highest in the whole zoo," said Tim.
Then they saw a giraffe. She was higher still,
with her long neck.

She bent her head all the way down to see Topsy and Tim. "Hello up there," said Tim.

"Look!" said Tim. "Horses in football jerseys."
The zebras showed how they could kick.
One kicked another with his back hooves.
"We don't want those zebras at home," said Dad.
"They might kick us."

"Look! White teddy bears!"
said Topsy.

"Those are polar bears," said Mummy, "and they are very fierce."
"We won't take them home," said Tim.

A crowd of people hurried past Topsy and Tim.
"They are going to watch the lions being fed,"
said Mummy.
"Let's go too!" shouted Topsy and Tim.

To the lions

The keeper brought huge lumps of meat for the lions.